Dear Parents and Teachers,

In an easy-reader format, **My Readers** introduce classic stories to children who are learning to read. Although favorite characters and time-tested tales are the basis for **My Readers**, the books tell completely new stories and are freshly and beautifully illustrated.

My Readers are available in three levels:

1 **Level One** is for the emergent reader and features repetitive language and word clues in the illustrations.

2 **Level Two** is for more advanced readers who still need support saying and understanding some words. Stories are longer with word clues in the illustrations.

3 **Level Three** is for independent, fluent readers who enjoy working out occasional unfamiliar words. The stories are longer and divided into chapters.

Encourage children to select books based on interests, not reading levels. Read aloud with children, showing them how to use the illustrations for clues. With adult guidance and rereading, children will eventually read the desired book on their own.

Here are some ways you might want to use this book with children:

- Talk about the title and the cover illustrations. Encourage the child to use these to predict what the story is about.
- Discuss the interior illustrations and try to piece together a story based on the pictures. Does the child want to change or adjust his first prediction?
- After children reread a story, suggest they retell or act out a favorite part.

My Readers will not only help children become readers, they will serve as an introduction to some of the finest classic children's books available today.

—LAURA ROBB
Educator and Reading Consultant

Thank you to Mary and Russ Hallowell
and the puppies of North Bend Retriever Kennels
for their friendly help.
—A. D.

SQUARE
FISH

An Imprint of Macmillan Children's Publishing Group

CARL AND THE PUPPIES. Copyright © 2011 by Alexandra Day.
All rights reserved.
Printed in June 2011 in China by Toppan Leefung Printing Ltd.,
Dongguan City, Guangdong Province.
For information, address Square Fish, 175 Fifth Avenue, New York, NY 10010.

Library of Congress Cataloging-in-Publication Data Available

ISBN 978-0-312-62482-8 (hardcover)
1 3 5 7 9 10 8 6 4 2

ISBN 978-0-312-62483-5 (paperback)
3 5 7 9 10 8 6 4 2

Book design by Patrick Collins/Véronique Lefèvre Sweet

Square Fish logo designed by Filomena Tuosto

First Edition: 2011

myreadersonline.com
mackids.com

This is a Level 1 book

LEXILE: 180L

CARL and the PUPPIES

story and pictures by
Alexandra Day

SQUARE
FISH

Macmillan Children's Publishing Group
New York

One of Carl's friends
needs help.
Who can it be?

It is Mama Dog and
her puppies,
Pete, Polly, and Molly.

Mama Dog is very tired.

She needs a nap.

Carl will take the puppies
for a walk.
Mama Dog will rest.

Carl says,

"Follow me, puppies."

Pete sees a butterfly.
Polly likes the flowers.

"No digging, Molly!"
says Carl.

Pete finds a skateboard.

Watch out, everybody!

Molly finds a frog.

What a surprise!

Polly runs ahead.

Where is Polly?

Here she is!

Pete wants the red ball.

It is hard to reach.

Uh, oh.

Pete is stuck.

Carl opens the gate
so Pete can get out.

The puppies want
to run down the hill

and tumble.

The puppies finally get tired.

Carl gives them a ride home.

Mama Dog had a nice nap.

She is glad to see the puppies.

Now, Carl needs a nap.
What a good dog, Carl.